MATCHDAY PROGRAMME

This jotter belongs to:

_____

© Scripture Union 2007
First published 2007

ISBN 978 1 84427 333 1

Scripture Union, 207–209 Queensway, Bletchley, Milton Keynes, MK2 2EB
Email: info@scriptureunion.org.uk
Website: www.scriptureunion.org.uk

Scripture Union Australia, Locked Bag 2, Central Coast Business Centre, MSW 2252, Australia
Website: www.scriptureunion.org.au

Scripture Union USA, PO Box 987, Valley Forge, PA 19482, USA
Website: www.scriptureunion.org

The selections from the books of Genesis and John are taken from the Contemporary English Version © American Bible Society. Anglicisations © British and Foreign Bible Society 1996. Published by HarperCollinsPublishers and used with kind permission.

British Cataloguing-in-Publication Data
A catalogue record of this book is available from the British Library.

Cover design by Kevin Wade, kwgraphicdesign
Cover and internal illustrations by Adrian Barclay

Scripture Union is an international Christian charity working with churches in more than 130 countries, providing resources to bring the good news of Jesus Christ to children, young people and families and to encourage them to develop spiritually through the Bible and prayer.

As well as our network of volunteers, staff and associates who run holidays, church-based events and school Christian groups, we produce a wide range of publications and support those who use our resources through training programmes.

MATCHDAY PROGRAMME

Welcome to your Matchday Programme! Here you'll find loads of stuff about Jesus: read from Luke's book all about Jesus (you can find the whole of Luke's book in the Bible) and do activities to help you find out more about him. At the end of Champion's Challenge you'll have a great reminder of everything you did, everything you heard and everything you discovered about Jesus!

Luke's Gospel ('Gospel' means 'book about the good news of Jesus') is split into 24 chapters. The chapter numbers are the big numbers. Each chapter is split into smaller verses. The verse numbers are the small numbers that appear in the story. Whenever you read a Bible, it works like that. Sometimes you will see a Bible verse written like this: Luke 9:23. Here is how you tell which verse to read:

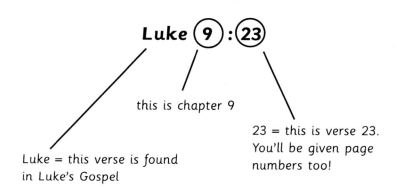

Luke (9) : (23)

this is chapter 9

Luke = this verse is found in Luke's Gospel

23 = this is verse 23. You'll be given page numbers too!

ON YOUR MARKS

Luke kicks off his story about Jesus right at the beginning! In the first two chapters, he tells the story of Jesus' birth, you know – the Christmas story! If you've got a whole Bible you could read the story for yourself, but if you turn to page 5 you can find a snapshot of the story there. At Champion's Challenge, you'll hear from Luke's book about different things Jesus did: he chose his squad, he trained the people who came to listen to him, he healed many people, he encouraged his squad and he performed miracles! At the end of the club, you'll also hear about something very special that Jesus did...

So, on your marks and get set to hear more about Jesus!

JESUS IS BORN!

LUKE 2:1–7

[1] About that time Emperor Augustus gave orders for the names of all the people to be listed in record books. [2] These first records were made when Quirinius was governor of Syria.

[3] Everyone had to go to their own home town to be listed. [4] So Joseph had to leave Nazareth in Galilee and go to Bethlehem in Judea. Long ago Bethlehem had been King David's home town, and Joseph went there because he was from David's family.

[5] Mary was engaged to Joseph and travelled with him to Bethlehem. She was soon going to have a baby, [6] and while they were there, [7] she gave birth to her firstborn son. She dressed him in baby clothes and laid him on a bed of hay, because there was no room for them in the inn.

JESUS NAMES HIS SQUAD

Jesus chose a group of people to help him. They were to learn from him and be his team!

LUKE 6:12–16

12 About that time Jesus went off to a mountain to pray, and he spent the whole night there. 13 The next morning he called his disciples together and chose twelve of them to be his apostles. 14 One was Simon, and Jesus named him Peter. Another was Andrew, Peter's brother. There were also James, John, Philip, Bartholomew, 15 Matthew, Thomas, and James the son of Alphaeus. The rest of the apostles were Simon, known as the Eager One, 16 Jude, who was the son of James, and Judas Iscariot, who later betrayed Jesus.

Spot the ten differences between these two pictures of Jesus' squad.

IN TRAINING

Jesus told many stories to train both his squad and the thousands of other people who came to listen to him. This story tells us how important it is to take notice of what Jesus says.

LUKE 6:46–49

46 Why do you keep on saying that I am your Lord, when you refuse to do what I say?

47 Anyone who comes and listens to me and obeys me 48 is like someone who dug down deep and built a house on solid rock. When the flood came and the river rushed against the house, it was built so well that it didn't even shake. 49 But anyone who hears what I say and doesn't obey me is like someone whose house wasn't built on solid rock. As soon as the river rushed against that house, it was smashed to pieces!

Under the picture of the wise man, write down everything that Jesus says is wise and under the foolish man, write down everything he says is foolish.

Why do you think it's important to listen to Jesus and do what he says? If possible, ask your Team Captain and the rest of your team what they think.

BUILDING ON ROCK

In the story of the two builders, Jesus talked about people coming and listening to him and obeying him. What kind of instructions do you think Jesus wants us to obey? What sort of things might Jesus want us to do to show we're obeying him? Chat with your Team Captain and the rest of your group and write your ideas on the bricks of this house, which has been built on rock!

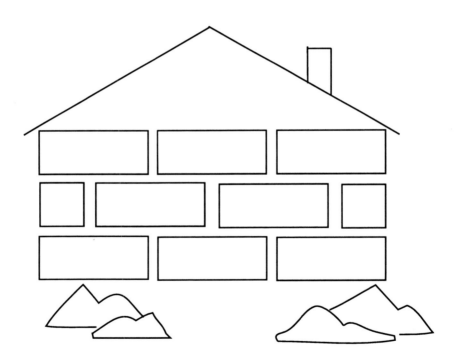

THAT'S IMPOSSIBLE!

In today's Bible story, Jesus does something which is absolutely amazing – you might even think it was impossible!

Write down anything that you think is impossible.

Then compare your answers to the others in your team!

STRONG FAITH!

Read this story where Jesus does something amazing!

LUKE 7:1–10

¹ After Jesus had finished teaching the people, he went to Capernaum. ² In that town an army officer's servant was sick and about to die. The officer liked this servant very much.

³ And when he heard about Jesus, he sent some Jewish leaders to ask him to come and heal the servant.

⁴ The leaders went to Jesus and begged him to do something. They said, "This man deserves your help! ⁵ He loves our nation and even built us a meeting place." ⁶ So Jesus went with them.

When Jesus wasn't far from the house, the officer sent some friends to tell him, "Lord, don't go to any trouble for me! I am not good enough for you to come into my house. ⁷ And I am certainly not worthy to come to you. Just say the word, and my servant will get well. ⁸ I have officers who give orders to me, and I have soldiers who take orders from me. I can say to one of them, 'Go!' and he goes. I can say to another, 'Come!' and he comes. I can say to my servant, 'Do this!' and he will do it."

⁹ When Jesus heard this, he was so surprised that he turned and said to the crowd following him, "In all of Israel I've never found anyone with this much faith!"
¹⁰ The officer's friends returned and found the servant well.

Work out an action for each of the verses. Read the story again and do each of your actions at the right time! Use the space below to write or draw your actions:

Faith: you have faith when you believe in something and you don't need proof to believe in it!

STORMY WEATHER

Here's another story about faith (look at page 13 to find out what faith is). You won't hear this story at Champion's Challenge, but it's great, so get reading!

LUKE 8:22–25

22 One day, Jesus and his disciples got into a boat, and he said, "Let's cross the lake." They started out, 23 and while they were sailing across, he went to sleep.

Suddenly a storm struck the lake, and the boat started sinking. They were in danger.
24 So they went to Jesus and woke him up, "Master, Master! We are about to drown!" Jesus got up and ordered the wind and waves to stop. They obeyed, and everything was calm. 25 Then Jesus asked the disciples, "Don't you have any faith?"

But they were frightened and amazed. They said to each other, "Who is this? He can give orders to the wind and the waves, and they obey him!"

The men in Jesus' squad were in trouble. They knew all about sailing – a lot of them used to go sailing every day because they were fishermen. They realised the storm was a big and dangerous one, and they were afraid. But they seemed to have forgotten all the amazing (even impossible) stuff that Jesus had done. It was as if they didn't know who Jesus was!

After Jesus had made everything calm, he asked them, 'Don't you have any faith?' He was asking them if they needed proof to believe in him. Read the Bible story again. Imagine you are caught in a dangerous storm and Jesus makes the storm stop. How would you answer the question, 'Who is this?'

Write or draw your thoughts on the waves here.

GET PACKING!

In this outline of a suitcase, write or draw all the things you would need to go on a long journey.

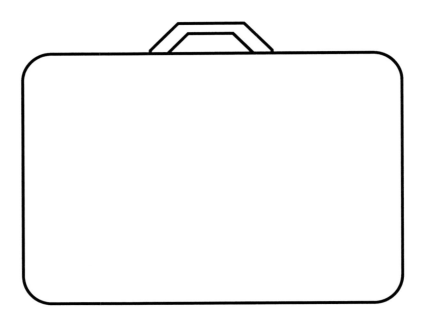

TELL THE GOOD NEWS!

Jesus encourages his team-mates to go and share the good news about himself. Underline all the things the disciples are NOT to take with them.

LUKE 9:1–6

[1] Jesus called together his twelve apostles and gave them complete power over all demons and diseases. [2] Then he sent them to tell about God's kingdom and to heal the sick. [3] He told them, "Don't take anything with you! Don't take a walking stick or a travelling bag or food or money or even a change of clothes. [4] When you are welcomed into a home, stay there until you leave that town. [5] If people won't welcome you, leave the town and shake the dust from your feet as a warning to them."

[6] The apostles left and went from village to village, telling the good news and healing people everywhere.

DISCIPLES' MAZE

Help Bartholomew and Simon to get to the two towns and then back to Jesus.

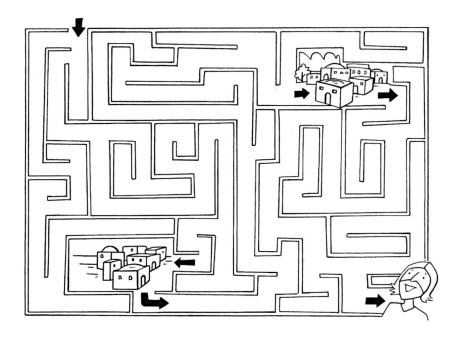

HALF-TIME SNACK

We're halfway through the club; it's time for a half-time snack. Try this recipe out at home with someone who looks after you – it's really simple!

What you need:

Three fish fingers

Two slices of bread

Butter or margarine

Brown sauce or ketchup

What you do:

Cook the fish fingers according to the instructions on the packet (make sure a grown-up helps you with this). While they are cooking, spread the two slices with butter, margarine or sauce – use whatever you like! When the fish fingers are ready, put them on top of one slice of bread and then place the other slice of bread on top to make a sandwich. Cut the sandwich in half and share with the grown-up who helped you.

How many people do you think you could feed with your sandwich?

SNACK FOR 5,000!

LUKE 9:10–17

¹⁰ The apostles came back and told Jesus everything they had done. He then took them with him to the village of Bethsaida, where they could be alone. ¹¹ But a lot of people found out about this and followed him. Jesus welcomed them. He spoke to them about God's kingdom and healed everyone who was sick.

¹² Late in the afternoon the twelve apostles came to Jesus and said, "Send the crowd to the villages and farms around here. They need to find a place to stay and something to eat. There is nothing in this place. It is like a desert!"

¹³ Jesus answered, "You give them something to eat."

But they replied, "We have only five small loaves of bread and two fish. If we are going to feed all these people, we will have to go and buy food." ¹⁴ There were about five thousand men in the crowd.

Jesus said to his disciples, "Tell the people to sit in groups of fifty." ¹⁵ They did this, and all the people sat down. ¹⁶ Jesus took the five loaves and the two fish. He looked up towards heaven and blessed the food. Then he broke the bread and fish and handed them to his disciples to give to the people.

¹⁷ Everyone ate all they wanted. What was left over filled twelve baskets.

ALL FULL UP

Fill in the gaps, using the Bible passage on page 21.

Jesus took the disciples to _____ where they could be
_____ (verse 10).

Lots of people _____ where Jesus was going and
_____ him (verse 11).

The disciples told Jesus to tell the crowd to go to the
local _____ and _____ to get food (verse 12).

Jesus told the disciples to feed the crowd, but the
disciples only had five _____ and two _____ (verse
13).

There were _____ men in the crowd (verse 14).

Jesus looked up to _____ and _____ the food (verse
16).

Everyone had enough and there were _____ baskets
left over (verse 17)!

WHAT DO YOU THINK?

Here are some words you might want to use to describe what you think of Jesus so far. Circle the ones that are best for you. If the word you want isn't here, write it in a space.

Awesome

Complicated

Exciting

Strange

Loving

Powerful

Confusing

Scary

God

Amazing

Wise

Friendly

CHAMPION'S CHALLENGE

Can you work out the Champion's Challenge Learn and remember verse using the codebreaker?

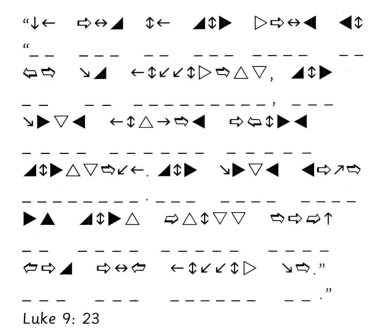

Luke 9: 23

JESUS' SQUAD

Here is the picture of Jesus and his squad again, but now we've written the names of the people underneath. He wants to choose us to be in his squad too. We'll find out more about that in Champion's Challenge!

Back row: Matthew, Philip, Bartholomew, Judas, Thomas, James

Front row: Simon, James, John, Jesus, Peter, Andrew, Jude

Would you like to be in his squad?

THE GOOD SAMARITAN

Another great story! Here Jesus is doing some more training, this time about who we should love.

LUKE 10:25–37

25 An expert in the Law of Moses stood up and asked Jesus a question to see what he would say. "Teacher," he asked, "what must I do to have eternal life?"

26 Jesus answered, "What is written in the Scriptures? How do you understand them?"

27 The man replied, "The Scriptures say, 'Love the Lord your God with all your heart, soul, strength, and mind.' They also say, 'Love your neighbours as much as you love yourself.'"

28 Jesus said, "You have given the right answer. If you do this, you will have eternal life."

29 But the man wanted to show that he knew what he was talking about. So he asked Jesus, "Who are my neighbours?"

30 Jesus replied:

As a man was going down from Jerusalem to Jericho, robbers attacked him and grabbed everything he had. They beat him up and ran off, leaving him half dead.

31 A priest happened to be going down the same road. But when he saw the man, he walked by on the other side.

^{32} Later a temple helper came to the same place. But when he saw the man who had been beaten up, he also went by on the other side.

^{33} A man from Samaria then came travelling along that road. When he saw the man, he felt sorry for him ^{34} and went over to him. He treated his wounds with olive oil and wine and bandaged them. Then he put him on his own donkey and took him to an inn, where he took care of him. ^{35} The next morning he gave the innkeeper two silver coins and said, "Please take care of the man. If you spend more than this on him, I will pay you when I return."

^{36} Then Jesus asked, "Which one of these three people was a real neighbour to the man who was beaten up by robbers?"

^{37} The teacher answered, "The one who showed pity." Jesus said, "Go and do the same!"

UP A TREE

Here is the story of a man called Zacchaeus. You won't meet him at Champion's Challenge, but his story is an important one! Read it and see what you think!

LUKE 19:1–10

¹ Jesus was going through Jericho, ² where a man named Zacchaeus lived. He was in charge of collecting taxes and was very rich. ³⁻⁴ Jesus was heading his way, and Zacchaeus wanted to see what he was like. But Zacchaeus was a short man and could not see over the crowd. So he ran ahead and climbed up into a sycamore tree.

⁵ When Jesus got there, he looked up and said,

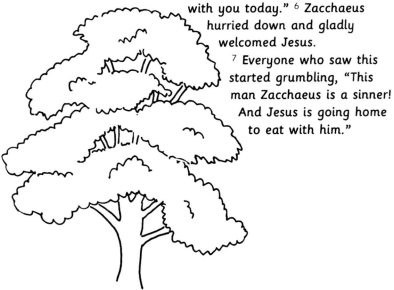

"Zacchaeus, hurry down! I want to stay with you today." ⁶ Zacchaeus hurried down and gladly welcomed Jesus.

⁷ Everyone who saw this started grumbling, "This man Zacchaeus is a sinner! And Jesus is going home to eat with him."

⁸ Later that day Zacchaeus stood up and said to the Lord, "I will give half of my property to the poor. And I will now pay back four times as much to everyone I have ever cheated."

⁹ Jesus said to Zacchaeus, "Today you and your family have been saved, because you are a true son of Abraham. ¹⁰ The Son of Man came to look for and to save people who are lost."

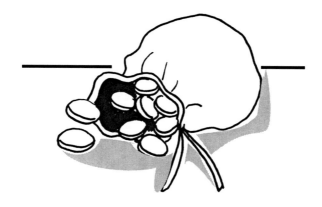

JESUS IS ARRESTED!

Jesus did so many good things – in fact he never did anything wrong! But he had enemies who didn't like the way he acted or the things he said. Eventually they found a way to arrest him.

LUKE 22:47–53

47 While Jesus was still speaking, a crowd came up. It was led by Judas, one of the twelve apostles. He went over to Jesus and greeted him with a kiss.

48 Jesus asked Judas, "Are you betraying the Son of Man with a kiss?"

49 When Jesus' disciples saw what was about to happen, they asked, "Lord, should we attack them with a sword?" 50 One of the disciples even struck at the high priest's servant with his sword and cut off the servant's right ear.

51 "Enough of that!" Jesus said. Then he touched the servant's ear and healed it.

52 Jesus spoke to the chief priests, the temple police, and the leaders who had come to arrest him. He said, "Why do you come out with swords and clubs and treat me like a criminal? 53 I was with you every day in the temple, and you didn't arrest me. But this is your time, and darkness is in control."

HAPPY OR SAD?

How do you think Jesus' squad, the disciples, were feeling when Jesus was arrested? Fill in these face shapes to show how they felt.

Verse 47

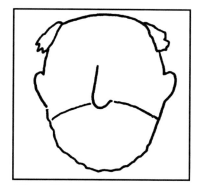

Verse 50

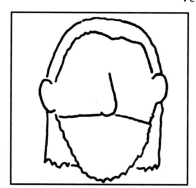

Verse 51

JESUS DIES

LUKE 23

◯ 1 Everyone in the council got up and led Jesus off to Pilate. 2 They started accusing him and said, "We caught this man trying to get our people to riot and to stop paying taxes to the Emperor. He also claims that he is the Messiah, our king."

3 Pilate asked Jesus, "Are you the king of the Jews?" "Those are your words," Jesus answered.

4 Pilate told the chief priests and the crowd, "I don't find him guilty of anything."

5 But they all kept on saying, "He has been teaching and causing trouble all over Judea. He started in Galilee and has now come all the way here."

6 When Pilate heard this, he asked, "Is this man from Galilee?" ◯ 7 After Pilate learnt that Jesus came from the region ruled by Herod, he sent him to Herod, who was in Jerusalem at that time.

8 For a long time Herod had wanted to see Jesus and was very happy because he finally had this chance. He had heard many things about Jesus and hoped to see him perform a miracle.

9 Herod asked him a lot of questions, but Jesus did not answer. 10 Then the chief priests and the teachers of the Law of Moses stood up and accused him of all kinds of bad things.

11 Herod and his soldiers made fun of Jesus and insulted him. They put a fine robe on him and sent him back to Pilate. 12 That same day Herod and Pilate became friends,

even though they had been enemies before this.

¹³ Pilate called together the chief priests, the leaders, and the people. ☉ ¹⁴ He told them, "You brought Jesus to me and said he was a troublemaker. But I have questioned him here in front of you, and I have not found him guilty of anything that you say he has done. ☉ ¹⁵ Herod didn't find him guilty either and sent him back. This man doesn't deserve to be put to death! ¹⁶⁻¹⁷ I will just have him beaten with a whip and set free."

☉ ¹⁸ But the whole crowd shouted, "Kill Jesus! Give us Barabbas!" ☉ ¹⁹ Now Barabbas was in jail because he had started a riot in the city and had murdered someone.

²⁰ Pilate wanted to set Jesus free, so he spoke again to the crowds. ²¹ But they kept shouting, "Nail him to a cross! Nail him to a cross!"

²² Pilate spoke to them a third time, "But what crime has he done? I have not found him guilty of anything for which he should be put to death. I will have him beaten with a whip and set free."

²³ The people kept on shouting as loud as they could for Jesus to be put to death. ²⁴ Finally, Pilate gave in. ²⁵ He freed the man who was in jail for rioting and murder, because he was the one the crowd wanted to be set free. Then Pilate handed Jesus over for them to do what they wanted with him.

²⁶ As Jesus was being led away, some soldiers grabbed hold of a man from Cyrene named Simon. He was coming in from the fields, but they put the cross on him and made him carry it behind Jesus.

²⁷ A large crowd was following Jesus, and in the crowd a

lot of women were crying and weeping for him. 28 Jesus turned to the women and said:
Women of Jerusalem, don't cry for me! Cry for yourselves and for your children.

29 Some day people will say, "Women who never had children are really fortunate!"

30 At that time everyone will say to the mountains, "Fall on us!" They will say to the hills, "Hide us!" 31 If this can happen when the wood is green, what do you think will happen when it is dry?

32 Two criminals were led out to be put to death with Jesus. 33 When the soldiers came to the place called "The Skull", they nailed Jesus to a cross. They also nailed the two criminals to crosses, one on each side of Jesus.

34-35 Jesus said, "Father, forgive these people! They don't know what they're doing." While the crowd stood there watching Jesus, the soldiers gambled for his clothes. The leaders insulted him by saying, "He saved others. Now he should save himself, if he really is God's chosen Messiah!"

36 The soldiers made fun of Jesus and brought him some wine. 37 They said, "If you are the king of the Jews, save yourself!"

38 Above him was a sign that said, "This is the King of the Jews."

39 One of the criminals hanging there also insulted Jesus by saying, "Aren't you the Messiah? Save yourself and save us!"

40 But the other criminal told the first one off, "Don't you fear God? Aren't you getting the same punishment as this man? 41 We got what was coming to us, but he didn't do anything wrong." 42 Then he said to Jesus, "Remember

me when you come into power!"

◌ 43 Jesus replied, "I promise that today you will be with me in paradise."

44 Around midday the sky turned dark and stayed that way until the middle of the afternoon. ◌ 45 The sun stopped shining, and the curtain in the temple split down the middle. ◌ 46 Jesus shouted, "Father, I put myself in your hands!" Then he died.

47 When the Roman officer saw what had happened, he praised God and said, "Jesus must really have been a good man!"

48 A crowd had gathered to see the terrible sight. Then after they had seen it, they felt brokenhearted and went home. 49 All Jesus' close friends and the women who had come with him from Galilee stood at a distance and watched.

◌ 50-51 There was a man named Joseph, who was from Arimathea in Judea. Joseph was a good and honest man, and he was eager for God's kingdom to come. He was also a member of the Jewish council, but he did not agree with what they had decided.

52 Joseph went to Pilate and asked for Jesus' body. 53 He took the body down from the cross and wrapped it in fine cloth. Then he put it in a tomb that had been cut out of solid rock and had never been used. 54 It was Friday, and the Sabbath was about to begin.

55 The women who had come with Jesus from Galilee followed Joseph and watched how Jesus' body was placed in the tomb. 56 Then they went to prepare some sweet-smelling spices for his burial. But on the Sabbath they rested, as the Law of Moses commands.

WHO DID WHAT?

Try answering these questions using Luke chapter 23 on pages 32 to 35. These verses are marked with a ☺.

Who was Jesus taken to first? (Verse 1)

What did Pilate do to Jesus after first meeting him? (Verse 7)

What had Jesus done wrong? (Verses 14 and 15)

Who did the crowd want Pilate to set free? (Verses 18 and 19)

Who was Jesus put to death with? (Verse 32)

What does Jesus promise one of the criminals? (Verse 43)

What happened when Jesus died? (Verses 45 and 46)

Who buried Jesus? (Verses 50 and 51)

JESUS IS ALIVE!

Winner

Jesus' death was not the end — something amazing was about to happen!

LUKE 24:1–35

¹ Very early on Sunday morning the women went to the tomb, carrying the spices that they had prepared. ² When they found the stone rolled away from the entrance, ³ they went in. But they did not find the body of the Lord Jesus, ⁴ and they did not know what to think.

Suddenly two men in shining white clothes stood beside them. ⁵ The women were afraid and bowed to the ground. But the men said, "Why are you looking in the place of the dead for someone who is alive? ⁶ Jesus isn't here! He has been raised from death. Remember that while he was still in Galilee, he told you, ⁷ 'The Son of Man will be handed over to sinners who will nail him to a cross. But three days later he will rise to life.'" ⁸ Then they remembered what Jesus had said.

⁹⁻¹⁰ Mary Magdalene, Joanna, Mary the mother of James, and some other women were the ones who had gone to the tomb. When they returned, they told the eleven apostles and the others what had happened. ¹¹ The apostles thought it was all nonsense, and they would not believe.

¹² But Peter ran to the tomb. And when he stooped down and looked in, he saw only the burial clothes. Then he returned, wondering what had happened.

¹³ That same day two of Jesus' disciples were going to the village of Emmaus, which was about eleven kilometres from Jerusalem. ¹⁴ As they were talking and thinking about what had happened, ¹⁵ Jesus came near and started walking along beside them. ¹⁶ But they did not know who he was.

¹⁷ Jesus asked them, "What were you talking about as you walked along?"

The two of them stood there looking sad and gloomy. ¹⁸ Then the one named Cleopas asked Jesus, "Are you the only person from Jerusalem who didn't know what was happening there these last few days?"

¹⁹ "What do you mean?" Jesus asked.

They answered, "Those things that happened to Jesus from Nazareth. By what he did and said he showed that he was a powerful prophet, who pleased God and all the people. ²⁰ Then the chief priests and our leaders had him arrested and sentenced to die on a cross. ²¹ We had hoped that he would be the one to set Israel free! But it has already been three days since all this happened. ²² Some women in our group surprised us. They had gone to the tomb early in the morning, ²³ but did not find the body of Jesus. They came back, saying that they had seen a vision of angels who told them that he is alive. ²⁴ Some men from our group went to the tomb and found it just as the women had said. But they didn't see Jesus either."

²⁵ Then Jesus asked the two disciples, "Why can't you understand? How can you be so slow to believe all that the prophets said? ²⁶ Didn't you know that the Messiah

would have to suffer before he was given his glory?" ²⁷ Jesus then explained everything written about himself in the Scriptures, beginning with the Law of Moses and the Books of the Prophets.

²⁸ When the two of them came near the village where they were going, Jesus seemed to be going further. ²⁹ They begged him, "Stay with us! It's already late, and the sun is going down." So Jesus went into the house to stay with them.

³⁰ After Jesus sat down to eat, he took some bread. He blessed it and broke it. Then he gave it to them. ³¹ At once they knew who he was, but he disappeared. ³² They said to each other, "When he talked with us along the road and explained the Scriptures to us, didn't it warm our hearts?" ³³ So they got up at once and returned to Jerusalem.

The two disciples found the eleven apostles and the others gathered together. ³⁴ And they learnt from the group that the Lord was really alive and had appeared to Peter. ³⁵ Then the disciples from Emmaus told what happened on the road and how they knew he was the Lord when he broke the bread.

FIND THE WORDS!

Track down these words from Luke 24:1–35 in this wordsearch!

W	S	P	I	C	E	S
H	A	E	S	L	E	E
I	T	T	T	E	A	M
T	O	E	O	O	T	M
E	M	R	N	P	L	A
I	B	R	E	A	D	U
V	E	J	E	S	U	S

WHITE

SPICES

STONE

TOMB

PETER   CLEOPAS

          BREAD

EAT

          EMMAUS   JESUS

Look at the letters left over – what word do they make?

BE PART OF JESUS' SQUAD!

When he died, Jesus took all the punishment that was meant for us – we can be forgiven for all the wrong things we have done. He came alive again so that we could be friends with God! And he wants us to be his friend – part of his squad – too!

If that's something you'd like to do, then talk to your Team Captain. You could say this prayer:

Jesus, I want to be your friend.
Thank you that you love me.
Thank you for living in the world and dying on a cross for me.
I'm sorry for all the wrong things I have done.
Please forgive me and let me be your friend.
Please let the Holy Spirit help me be like you.
Amen.

PERSONAL BEST!

At Champion's Challenge, you might set your own record in some challenges. Write down what your challenges are and then record your personal best in each one. Can you set a new personal best throughout the week?

Challenge 1:

Personal best:_____

New personal best:_____

New personal best:_____

Challenge 2:

Personal best:_____

New personal best:_____

New personal best:_____

Challenge 3:

Personal best:_____

New personal best:_____

New personal best:_____

Challenge 4:

Personal best:_____

New personal best:_____

New personal best:_____

Jesus wants us to be as good as we can be, so well done on your personal bests! When we're on Jesus' squad, we can make a difference whatever our talents!

A HELPER

Champion

This is the start of Luke's second book, Acts, which is about what Jesus' squad did after he had gone back to heaven. But before he went, Jesus promised a helper – the Holy Spirit.

ACTS 1:1–8

¹ Theophilus, I first wrote to you about all that Jesus did and taught from the very first ² until he was taken up to heaven. But before he was taken up, he gave orders to the apostles he had chosen with the help of the Holy Spirit.

³ For forty days after Jesus had suffered and died, he proved in many ways that he had been raised from death. He appeared to his apostles and spoke to them about God's kingdom.

⁴ While he was still with them, he said, "Don't leave Jerusalem yet. Wait here for the Father to give you the Holy Spirit, just as I told you he has promised to do. ⁵ John baptized with water, but in a few days you will be baptized with the Holy Spirit."

⁶ While the apostles were still with Jesus, they asked him, "Lord, are you now going to give Israel its own king again?"

⁷ Jesus said to them, "You don't need to know the time of those events that only the Father controls. ⁸ But the Holy Spirit will come upon you and give you power. Then you will tell everyone about me in Jerusalem, in all Judea, in Samaria, and everywhere in the world."

THE BEST BITS OF CHAMPION'S CHALLENGE

The funniest bit . . . .

The most interesting bit . . . .

The silliest bit . . . .

The bit I learnt about God . . . .

The bit I will remember . . . .

MY TEAM MATES!

Collect the names and doodles of your team and Team Captain!

Lightning Source UK Ltd.
Milton Keynes UK
UKOW031506270613

212840UK00001B/31/P

9 781844 273331